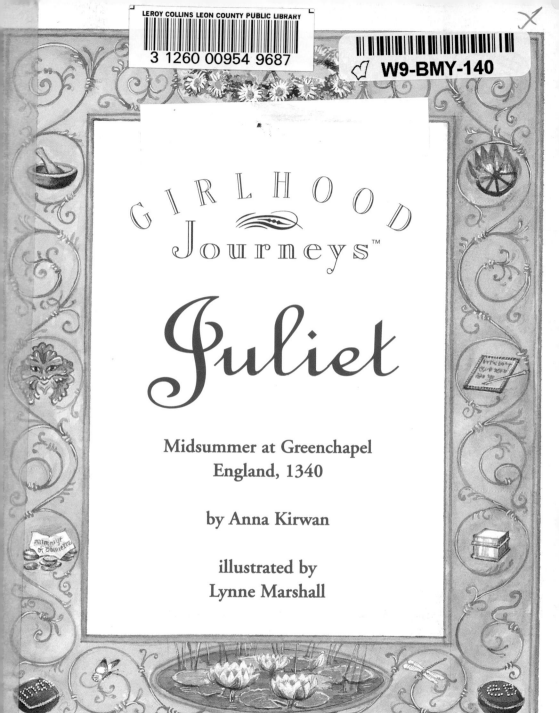

GIRLHOOD
JOURNEYS™

Juliet

Midsummer at Greenchapel
England, 1340

by Anna Kirwan

illustrated by
Lynne Marshall

GIRLHOOD JOURNEYS™ COLLECTION

ALADDIN PAPERBACKS

25 Years of Magical Reading

ALADDIN PAPERBACKS
EST. 1972

For the boys: my sons, Max and Robin;
my nephews, Paul, Christopher, Alexander, and Jacob;
my special friends, Jesse, Sam, Daniel,
Mathew, Tom, Dmitri, and Jeff.

Grateful acknowledgment is made to Corbis-Bettman, for the illustration on page 65, and to The Illustrated London News Picture Library, for the illustration on page 66. The photograph on page 68 is from *The English Mediaeval House* by Margaret Wood (Studio Editions Ltd., London).

First Aladdin Paperbacks edition December 1997

Aladdin Paperbacks
An imprint of Simon & Schuster Children's Publishing Division
1230 Avenue of the Americas
New York, NY 10020

Designed by Wendy Letven Design
The text of this book was set in Garamond.
Printed and bound in Hong Kong
10 9 8 7 6 5 4 3 2 1

Library of Congress Cataloging-in-Publication Data
Kirwan, Anna.
Juliet: Midsummer at Greenchapel, England, 1340 / by Anna Kirwan ;
 illustrated by Lynne Marshall.
— 1st Aladdin Paperbacks ed.
p. cm. — (Girlhood journeys)
Summary: On the day before Midsummer Eve in England in 1340, eleven-year-old Juliet accompanies Gil on a trip to get medicine for a wounded falcon while hoping to arrive home on time for the fun.
ISBN 0-689-81560-3 (pbk.)
[1. Middle Ages—Fiction. 2. England—Fiction. 3. Festivals—Fiction. 4. Holidays—Fiction.] I. Marshall, Lynne, ill. II. Title. III. Series.
PZ7.K6395Jm 1997
[Fic]—dc21
97-24285
CIP
AC

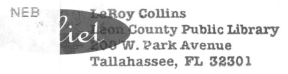

CONTENTS

TO THE READER

Certain sentences in "Mummy Powder," chapter 3 of *Midsummer at Greenchapel*, are written using authentic spellings of old-fashioned Middle English words. These spellings are taken from vocabulary used by the poet Chaucer in his *Canterbury Tales*, and are printed in **THIS TYPEFACE** in the story.

The words may look strange, but if you sound them out you can crack the Middle English "code." If you're not sure you've decoded the sentences correctly, complete translations appear in the Afterword.

MIDSUMMER EVE
MORNING

As it happened, Juliet Blackwell was in the knot garden and her mouth was full of pins when the Green Wolf Boys came to take Jehan and Joseph. Even at eleven, Juliet was as excited as the five-year-old pages were—and they were bouncy as crickets this morning. Everyone at Greenchapel was looking forward to the Midsummer feast day of St. John.

The new hay stood sweet and flower-studded, ready for cutting, and the first few fields had been mown already. All the countryside was about to celebrate the shortest night of the year. There would be bonfires, music, and dancing, and merry companies of trade guild members and scholars would stage contests and plays.

Juliet was maid-in-waiting to her best friend, Lady Marguerite D'Arsy. They had not been staying at Greenchapel Manor long enough to know many of the tradespeople by name, but they did know most of the crew of young nobles called the Green Wolves. Lately, the girls had been teaching the twin page boys to recognize who was who, so they'd be able to serve the Green Wolves by carrying messages back and forth.

"Sir Jerome will be your captain," Juliet reminded them, "now that you're big enough to help the fellows get everything ready for the bonfire." Sir Jerome de Gonfalon was the young man Marguerite was betrothed to marry in a few years, when she'd turn fifteen.

"Tell me their names again," Joseph coaxed. He was entirely the opposite of his brother—he talked and listened well. Jehan was more rowdy, all knees-to-nose tumbling and climbing, likely to point or gesture instead of using words.

"Well, Randall Swynford, Peggy's brother. He's the one with the cap you said looks like a pie." Marguerite set down the snippet of velvet she was sewing so she could count on her fingers. "The Tuftons, Aimery and Eustache. . . ." Aside, to Juliet, Marguerite murmured, "I think Sir Aimery is very taken with Enid. What do you think? I wonder if her mother knows."

Juliet had just joined two seams, and she had several straight pins clamped between her pursed lips, so she could only raise her eyebrows a bit and shrug to answer Marguerite. But she had been noticing how much the Tuftons seemed to be around when she and Marguerite and their friend, Enid Buckler, were together. It could be Sir Aimery was dancing atten-dance on their heiress friend.

"And that Eustache—what a courtly swain!" Marguerite went on. "All the poetry he recites! What was it he said to you the other day, Juliet?"

Juliet took the pins from between her lips and pieced together the next seam she had to sew. She was making costumes for the twins to wear for the parts they were going to act in the Green Wolves' miracle play, probably about some saint's life.

"It was just a line from a French song," Juliet said, embarrassed. She paused to brush away a few quince-blossom petals that had fallen on her new summer gown. "About me being a maid-in-waiting." Eustache was quite friendly to her, even though she was a com-moner. And he really did seem to have some song lyric or elegant phrase for everything on which he needed to remark. He was very learned, for a four-teen-year-old. But Enid Buckler had been known to mimic delicately his way of letting his gaze drift upward and humming whatever came before the line he was trying to remember. Marguerite and Enid hadn't actually said so, but Juliet could tell they thought Eustache was rather full of himself some-times.

"And how did the line go?"

"Oh, something about, 'Honor comes from serving ladies of such quality . . .' I don't remember the rest."

"Perhaps he'll want to leap the bonfire and dance

with you this eve," Marguerite said kindly. "At a party, he'll not mind your sturdy, un-French lineage."

Juliet started stitching her seam. She had thought she might be too young for Sir Eustache; she hadn't been thinking about her lineage. She was certainly too young for a suitor, if he weren't a noble. Commoners like Juliet and her friend Gil Falconer had to work hard for years to be able to marry. It was the nobility who received the sacrament of marriage young and served the royalty.

As Juliet sewed, she removed the pins holding the green fabric and put them back, one by one, between her lips. She knew it wasn't the safest way to work, but Marguerite and Enid had been making little Midsummer Night fortune-telling pincushions. Girls in noble society placed them under their pillows on that night so they'd dream of their futures. A velvet cushion had to have a maiden's initials pricked into it in silver pins— and, between *M.D'A.* and *E.B.,* there were not a lot of pins left over. Juliet was trying to keep track of as many as she could despite Jehan's having accidentally overturned her sewing basket into the marigold bed a few moments earlier. She planned to start sewing her own velvet cushion just as soon as she finished her task of sewing for the boys. She usually remembered her dreams, but things often happened in them she did not understand. If you *knew* a dream was about your future, she thought, that would help you to . . . .

Jehan was fidgeting from one foot to the other. He was restless having to have his costume sewed, and tried on, and sewed more.

"And, of course," Marguerite went on, smiling at Jehan and Joseph, "these two savage brothers. They will make good Green Wolves, I'll wager. They certainly do enough howling."

Jehan growled and clambered around a large urn planted with golden honeysuckle. Clearly, he was close to the end of his willingness to stand still and be good. Juliet was used to her own little brother, Alban, acting this way. *Another moment*, she thought, *and he'll be down on his hands and knees, all daubed with dirt and dew.*

"They're taking advantage of Juliet's patience," Lady Enid said as she strolled back to the group by the mossy walk. Her hands were full of daisies and verbena she'd just gathered. "What nice hoods she's making for you! You'll look like Robin of Sherwood!"

Sir Jerome sauntered into the garden just then. He was wearing the green tunic of his own costume, but carrying his Wolf helmet.

"We'll take these young knaves," he sallied, tagging Jehan on the shoulder. "Into thieves' dens and dark places. What do you say, lads, shall we go find some bones to burn? Some rags and straw and branches and such? Jack of the Greenwood wants your best hard work for his bonfire—and the worst stinking rubbish. Are you ready to come with us? Are they ready to go, my Lady?"

He bent over and kissed Marguerite's hand.

Jack of the Greenwood was what everyone called the big leafy giant in feast-day plays and dances. When Juliet was little, her father, Wystan Blackwell, had told her about Jack o' th' Green liking fires; Juliet remembered thinking Jack must be the bravest of all knights, to be so much like a tree, but not afraid of fire.

Juliet knotted her last thread carefully, three times, and snipped it off with Marguerite's silver shears before she let herself look up to see if Eustache Tufton had come with Jerome.

He had. He was there, dark hair and sparsely whiskered upper lip and surprising blue eyes. He turned toward her, looking at her, then quickly away. Was he flirting with her? Would a courtly swain flirt with a maiden of her age? Had he noticed her new gown? It was part of her wages to have new clothes. Hers were plainer than Marguerite's and Enid's, but they were more elegant than she'd had before. Had Eustache noticed she was not wearing the same old thing, for once?

"If Juliet's finished their costumes," Marguerite answered Jerome, "Joseph and Jehan have my leave to go with you."

Juliet turned Joseph's hood right side out and took the pins out of her mouth, looking for her ordinary, fortuneless pincushion to put them in for the nonce.

She found it under the marigolds.

"They're ready," she said. Jerome grabbed up Jehan and set him atop his shoulders. Jehan howled joyously.

"Where are you taking them to scavenge?" Juliet asked Jerome. "My brother Tom said he'd save you the kitchen bones, even if the lads from the White Hill team come yelling first."

"The kitchen, then," Jerome agreed.

"I have been composing a poetic song," Eustache announced to no one in particular. "It is about St. Edmund, the king of East Anglia, getting shot with arrows and cut to pieces by the Danes, and about how no one could find his head until a wolf scavenged the field and found it under a bush.

"It is a song," he added, "both sad and glorious."

Juliet caught Marguerite and Enid exchanging grins, and she could imagine what her older brother Tom would call Eustache—a rooster, maybe. A strutting pigeon. That was what he had called Randall. But then, Juliet remembered, Tom couldn't compose a polite poem about a saint's head *or* speak French, could he? So what use was his opinion? Just because he was your big brother, it wasn't as if he saw things the way Father would. He was probably just envious.

Enid gently changed the subject back to the Green Wolf Boys' quest.

"The oaks behind the chapel had a lot of tent worms this spring," she observed. "The friar cut quite a pile of branches. But, to collect them, you'll have to

get there before the joiners or any of the others do. . . .
Heigh, look," she interrupted herself. "Here's Gil, with
the feathers to stuff our good-luck cushions."

"Ho, Falconer," Jerome called to the boy in russet
livery who was striding up the lily-edged walk. Gil
was Juliet and Marguerite's oldest friend, from
Rosebriar. His family's work was keeping the hunting
hawks and falcons for Marguerite's father and their
liege lord, Baron Hubert. "We want all the dirty molt-
feathers and straw from the mews, as well," Jerome
informed him. "Our bonfire will be tallest this year,
by all the saints."

"Feathers, aye, sir," Gil said, saluting the noble
lads and ladies by tugging at the mop of hair that
fell over his forehead. "This sack is full of clean
feathers, as Master Jehan came and bid me gather.
Besides the hawks' down, I added swans' down from
the reeds by the River Witham. But, as to the bonfire—" Gil paused a moment, and sighed. He did
not usually have to say so much among court folk,
and he was a quiet fellow, anyway, tending to think
several things before he spoke once. "The wool
guildsmen came while I was down by the river," he
explained with unfestive soberness, "and begged the
straw from a cadge-boy. They're starting their fire
this year with a great big basketwork statue of St.
John with his lamb, and they took all the birds'
litter to kindle it, more woe to me. That is my other
reason to be here, sir. There is a troublesome errand
I must pursue."

"Why, what's the trouble, Gil?" Marguerite asked with concern.

"When they took the straw, they meant to be helpful, and they saw the stack of fresh turf pieces I'd brought over to the mews for my birds. They enjoy the grass floor now, while they're molting. The falcons, I mean, not the Woolly Boys. But the boys took out the straw, and, seeing I wasn't there, they themselves spread the turf around the birds' blocks and perches—which was meant as a kindness. Yet it was not well, for one of the pieces of turf was dug from a weasel's warren, and the weasel bit Baron Hubert's gyr, Amfortas. When I came back, there was hardly anything of the weasel left, and Amfortas had a big wound oozing blood and water."

Eustache smiled at Juliet, and flicked a hand at the wolf-fur trim of his costume to remove a bit of down that had escaped from the sack Gil handed over to Enid.

"How does that song go. . . ?" he half whispered. *"When Juno sendeth the hawker woe, who, splashing, at her swans doth go . . ."*

Everyone could hear him recite. Juliet saw Gil flush—with embarrassment or anger, she didn't know which. Eustache was jesting, yet Juliet knew the falcons were Gil's responsibility when his father was away. A wounded bird was not a jesting matter for Gil. But he squared his shoulders and went on speaking to Marguerite and Jerome, keeping his back half turned away from Eustache—and Juliet.

"So, now," he said stolidly, "I must go to the

apothecary Jervis Towhee, at Lincoln, to get the proper medicine. And I must go soon, so as not to be on the road still by nightfall."

"Take my horse," Sir Jerome told him promptly. "You'll be back in good time."

"Here's three shillings to pay the apothecary," Marguerite said, reaching into the pocket she wore beneath her surcoat.

"Three shillings won't be enough, my Lady," Gil said uncomfortably. Juliet thought he must not like asking for money in front of everyone, as if he were a beggar, and not a freeman and a falconer. "This medicine is dearly bought. Merchants bring it from the East."

"Then take twenty shillings, and make a bargain as you see fit," Marguerite instructed, handing him the coins. "Is there anything else?"

"Aye," Gil said, and Juliet saw him flush again. After a moment, he went on in his soft, measured voice. "Towhee cannot hear nor speak. A person cannot talk freely with him, but must write his questions, and read Towhee's advice."

So that was it. He did not say it, but everyone there knew: Gil could not read.

And Juliet saw all the Midsummer Eve's preparations and fun around Greenchapel Manor suddenly bolt beyond her grasp, like a falcon flying away over a hedge. She knew what had to happen next. She was a maid-in-waiting, a commoner, not one of the nobles. But she could read and write.

"I'll go with you, Gil," she said. ❖

THE ROAD TO
LINCOLN

"Have you seen my Apple around here today?" Gil asked the stable boy, Harry, who was pulling a halter over the long ears of a donkey named Argent. It had been agreed that Juliet should ride Lark, Jerome's palfrey, because it was well behaved.

"You've asked me that three times already this morning," Harry answered. "No. I have not seen your dog, nor any of the dogs, for a while. The Miller's Boys were around at the crack of dawn, whipping those little fire wheels of theirs off the ends of sticks, practicing how far they could send them. My pup got his tail singed—it put a right scare into him. Perhaps your spaniel went off for the same reason—heigh, watch that, you crow's meat!" The last remark was to Argent, who had jerked her head back while Harry was holding the bridle, pulling him off balance. Harry tossed the reins over a hitching rail and turned his attention toward the saddle blanket.

"Apple never goes far," Juliet said. Gil's cheerful

little dog was her own favorite, too, and any other time she would have been upset that she was missing. But Juliet was already mounted on Lark, who had carried her on many a ride with Marguerite. If Gil took any time to hunt for Apple again, they'd never get to Lincoln and back before nightfall.

Juliet felt a little guilty for her impatience, but, after all, she hushed her conscience, when you were in service your lord's errands had to come first, even if it made a grumpy gyrkin more important than sweet little Apple, with her ears like silk just waiting for you to whistle.

"She's going to have those pups anytime, though," Gil worried. "I'll not be able to find her once it's dark."

Argent sidled toward Harry and plucked with her teeth at a pouch he wore on his belt.

"So that's what you want, eh?" he said. "Here, Falconer, this is how you keep this sorry jennet sweet." He opened the pouch and took out a brown lump Argent quickly gobbled out of his hand. "Give her a bit of this ginger-and-fennel bread, and she'll forget being stubborn and move right along."

Tediously, Gil pulled his pack around in front of him and began unbuckling and unstrapping it. Juliet could see that he was worried to distraction, but she thought she'd never seen him do anything so maddeningly slowly.

"Here, I'll take it," she volunteered quickly. "I can put it right into my pocket." The gingerbread Harry handed her was stale and hard, but it still smelled spicy. *At least we'll be able to get the animals moving,* she thought. *I wonder if it'd work on Gil.*

In truth, it only seemed a long time before they were on the rutted road away from Greenchapel, clipping briskly through the village beyond the manor's orchards. They passed cottage after cottage where folk were at work binding bundles of straw onto old cartwheels and broomsticks, preparing for evening. Before the sun was well down, the country around about would be dappled with fires. The broomsticks would become torches, and wheels would be trundled up every hill worth the name, set ablaze, and rolled down gloriously into the green fields. The cottagers would parade their newly sheared sheep and darling lambs, their cattle and pigs and oxen, through the billows of black smoke, because the Midsummer fires could chase off every kind of trouble—fleas, sickness, fairy mischief, or the devil. Marguerite and Jerome, perhaps Enid and Aimery—and certainly Eustache—would go about from one bonfire to another, singing and dancing to "Daisy Chain" and "Thread the Needle."

If we're not back from Lincoln, Juliet told herself,

no one will wait for us. They probably won't even notice. No one is noticing me today—or my new gown.

She glanced sideways at Gil. They had gone far enough away from the stable and mews that he had stopped peering every which way for Apple, and now he was just staring glumly at a spot between Argent's ears. He looked too somber to be riding along in the merry sunshine, she thought.

But, after all, his holiday was slipping away from him, just as her own was. It occurred to her, for the thousandth time, that not even the kindest of her noble friends, not even Marguerite and Jerome, gave much thought to how common people and serfs worked and worked, the whole year around. Somehow, it had never bothered her much when she was back in the cottage at Rosebriar, helping her mother and father with Alban and the baby, Eleanor. As much as she loved being at court with Marguerite, sometimes it just stabbed her heart to be away from her real home. Perhaps, she thought, it was harder for Gil to work in the mews when his father, Piers Falconer, was away at one of the baron's other manors.

Eustache certainly didn't understand that, she thought, or he would never have made fun of Gil. Juliet felt her own resentment slipping from her, and she decided to put it aside entirely. Perhaps if she could get Gil talking, he would feel better. She was sure *she* would. The day was really lovely (if only they wouldn't miss the bonfire dancing!), and journeys were much more pleasant if you had stories to shorten the road.

"Eustache said the joiners are putting on a play about Sir Gawain and the Holy Grail and the Green Knight," she began. Gil grunted, but didn't say anything. Juliet tried again. "So, you said the Woolly Boys are burning a wicker statue of St. John?"

"Aye. Harry says they're none so happy about it, though," Gil replied.

"Why not?"

"Oh, he says here at Greenchapel their guild always used to take the prizes in the high-jumping contests. They've got a whole family, the Harbys, nine of 'em, can jump like water on a griddle. But this year, His Majesty's law is still against any contests except shooting. There won't be any prizes for jumping nor running nor swords nor jousting."

"I wish His Majesty had not made it the law, no games but longbows," Juliet complained. She and Gil both had always liked running for sport. A person did not need armor or equipment—anyone could do it, anytime, except for maids-in-waiting when people were watching. "Goodness knows, there are already enough other ways a person can get sentenced to beheading."

"Sir Aimery says King Edward is a long-sighted warrior," Gil informed her. "Every Englishman should be useful with his longbow. The King of France never had archers as good as England, anyway. But now that His Majesty is squabbling with his cousins the Crowned Heads, we had better have even better." Gil shrugged.

Juliet flicked a big, blue horsefly off Lark's neck, and tried not to think about the bouquets of blue larkspur folks liked to bring to the Midsummer bonfires to strengthen their eyes. Gil still had not cracked a smile. She wasn't doing enough smiling herself, she thought restlessly. What was there over which they *could* feel good cheer?

"At least," she started, "with this fine medicine, Amfortas will heal quickly. . . ."

Gil shook his head and sighed.

"Now he's molting and not so fair to look upon, his ugly temperament shows more. What a brute he is! And I just don't fancy putting this remedy on him when we do get it. He'll probably go for my eyes. Besides, he's off his feed. I gave him the usual fare, eels and mice—and even jackdaw hearts—but he does not like anything good for him. He's such a nasty-tempered old devil."

What *was* it about today? Things moved from bad to worse! "Don't be talking about the devil, Gil," Juliet said hastily. "The fires aren't lit, yet. It's not safe."

Gil looked frightened for a moment, too, and crossed himself. It was true, a soul couldn't be too careful.

But at this rate, Juliet thought, she'd *never* get a smile out of Gil. She could see she'd best change the subject yet again. "What sort of herb is it, anyway, that we have to go all the way to Lincoln?"

Gil felt at his belt for the pouch that held

Marguerite's coins and took from it a scrap of parchment he held out to Juliet to read. "My dad had that written out for me before he went off with Sir Pepin. He said, in case grave harm came to one of the birds, ask Master Jervis Towhee in Lincoln if it be called for."

Argent did not want Lark to come too close, so it took a moment before Juliet could catch hold of the note and examine it. "*Mummy powder of Damietta,*" she said, puzzled. "What's that?"

"My dad says it's better than ash of seaweed for a wet wound," Gil said. Something about the way he said it made Juliet think he was avoiding a direct answer. "It's not exactly an herb," he added after a moment.

"But what *is* it?" she insisted.

Gil mumbled his reply. "It's made from dead men's heads."

"*What . . . !*" Juliet was so horrified she almost fell off Lark. "What are you talking about!"

"Not Englishmen's heads," Gil amended quickly. "It's from Egypt. They're heathens there." He struggled to explain. "They used to pickle their kings when they were dead, see, and wrap them up in their old bedclothes. And now, when they find one of these old kings and take hold of him, pieces fall off like a leper's nose and fingers, and turn to dust. And the dust is the best medicine to dry up an oozing sore. *Everyone* knows that," he added defensively.

"I never heard of such a thing!" Juliet told him, outraged.

"Well, it's the truth," Gil said stubbornly. "My dad says so."

Juliet stared bleakly out at the boggy meadow pond they were passing. The air was sweet with the scent of wild rose and yellow water lilies, and little blue dragonflies darted in and out of the grass, like darning needles. But Juliet's heart was hardly gladdened. Here it was, Midsummer Eve, when every witch, ghost, fairy, dragon, and greenycoat in the world was apt to be roaming about looking for souls to trouble. And not only were she and Gil going to miss the fun and safety of the bonfires—they were going to be wandering around carrying some dead heathen's powdered pickled nose and eyeballs with them!

This was not turning out to be the lovely, romantic Midsummer Eve she had pictured. What if she did have a new gown? They'd call the day blessed if they made it home neither bewitched nor elf-led. They'd be lucky if their holy-day clothes didn't get totally ruined. ❖

CHAPTER THREE

MUMMY POWDER

S teep Street in Lincoln climbed the long hill toward the cathedral, and it was here that Juliet and Gil found the house of Jervis Towhee. Its old-fashioned stone front sported three arched windows. The doorway was set deep into the wall, under a chimney that rose to a cone-shaped cap.

"It looks to be a rich man's house," Juliet said as she slid off Lark and looped the reins through an iron ring near the door jamb. But there was a sign mounted there as well, a plain wooden tile. "It says visitors should come right in," she added.

"He cannot hear a knock, anyway," Gil reminded Juliet. He climbed down from Argent's elegant, tall saddle and tied her quickly, avoiding her attempt to nip at his sleeve. "Harry came here once. He said Towhee has his storeroom and shop on the ground floor. The house was his grandfather's, back in old King Longshanks's time."

"Well, let us go in, and be done as soon as may be," Juliet said. "We still have to travel all the way back the way we came—and look how long the shadows already are by Great St. Hugh's Tower on the cathedral. It's getting late."

The corridor they entered was refreshingly cool after the dusty afternoon's ride and sweaty climb through the city. The shop door was on their right. Inside, an old man sat behind the tall counter, using a pestle to grind herbs in a wooden mortar. The counter and the shelves that lined the walls were cluttered with earthenware herb jars. The sharp, green scent of willow bark filled the room.

Jervis Towhee might have been the oldest man Juliet had ever seen. His face was so grayish and wrinkled, he looked as if he himself had bark instead of skin. Even the long locks of yellowish white hair that hung along his cheeks were rather like lank sprays of weeping willow.

He looked them over with shrewd interest, then pushed aside the mortar and pestle and reached for a wax-covered wooden tablet that was lying on the countertop. Taking a silver stylus from behind one ear, he scratched something into the soft surface of the tablet so the black wood showed through. He held it out for them to read.

"WHO SUFFRETH PEIN?" Juliet read his question.

"Write that it's a passager gyrkin, some two years of age, and well into its molt," Gil told her.

"I can't write all that," Juliet protested. "The tablet's not big enough, and I write too slowly—we haven't got all day. Besides, I'm not sure how to write 'gyrkin.' It's not in either of Marguerite's books." She thought for a moment and decided to do things the easiest way: She pointed to the crest on Gil's livery that marked him as one of Sir Pepin D'Arsy's men. The crest showed a falcon surrounded by a wreath of rosebriar.

At first, Jervis Towhee looked puzzled; then his expression cleared and he nodded.

"He understands," Gil said as the old man took back the tablet and used his hand to rub the wax smooth again before inscribing a new question: HOW GRETE BE HE?

"What difference does that make, great or small?" Gil asked when Juliet had read it to him. "His *wound* is big enough."

"When my mum makes up herb cures," Juliet informed him, "she has to know if they're for children or big people, so she won't make them too strong."

"Oh, I see," Gil said. "Well, Amfortas is not so brawny, for a gyr—he could be bigger. But now he's been in molt and not flying, he's soft and gone to fat. . . ."

Juliet had been rubbing out the apothecary's words. She took the stylus he held out to her and

wrote: **FAT NU NOUGHT BRAWNY.**

The old man nodded seriously and asked: **WHAT WILLE HE ETE?** Juliet smeared off the letters and studiously spelled: **JACKDAW HERTES AND ELES AND MYS.**

Jervis Towhee's eyebrows bunched together with dismay; but, then, Juliet remembered how disgusted Eustache and Enid had both been when they watched the falcons being fed one morning. She wrote: **HYM LIKETH HYT NOUGHT. HYT MAKETH HYM GRUCCHE.**

Towhee nodded, but still appeared troubled. **HOW BE HYS COLOUR?** he asked.

"He should be white with black markings," Gil instructed, "but now almost all his feathers are off, he's all flesh." Juliet wrote: **ALLE WHITE FALLYNGE OFF FLESSHE.**

When the apothecary read that, he drew in his breath with such alarm, Juliet thought he would drop the tablet. He waved a hand back and forth in front of him as if warning them off, took up the stylus as if he feared to touch it, and wrote hastily:

PRAYESTOW FOR MERCIE. THISE MANNE DARSY BE A LEPRE.

Juliet had read the words aloud to Gil before their meaning struck. Gil's mouth fell open in astonishment. Then, so did hers. They both swiveled to look at Towhee, then gazed back at the words on the tablet.

Then they burst out laughing.

"No! No! The *bird* on the crest," Gil exclaimed, forgetting Towhee couldn't hear him. "Not the *owner!*"

It took Juliet a few moments to clear the tablet and write: **NOUGHT SIR PEPIN. A WESEL BITEN OON HYS HAUKES.** (It might have taken less time to write it if she had not started giggling again when Gil said, "Wish he *were* a leper—maybe his beak'd fall off before I have to go near him again!")

Jervis Towhee, meanwhile, had been staring at them somewhat nervously. When he saw Juliet's new message, though, he tipped his own head to one side and laughed—at least, a thin smile reached across his face, and a whispery, rustling sound came from his lips.

Gil took out the piece of parchment and showed it to him. Towhee looked thoughtful, then nodded. He reached under the counter and brought out a leather coffret. Juliet and Gil saw the lid was carved with a picture of a unicorn dipping its horn

into a pool. Inside the coffret were three small tins like the ones pedlars used for rare spices such as pepper and sandalwood powder. Towhee took one out for them, then wrote on the tablet: **KEPESTOW DRYE THISE CURE.** When Gil poured out Marguerite's twenty shillings on the counter, Towhee took eleven. Gil nodded and put the rest back in his pouch, along with the tin.

Juliet wrote: **WIR YEVE THANKES.** "Shall we go now?" she asked Gil.

"Wait on it a minute more," Gil said. "Let's ask him how he came to be thus deaf and dumb."

"I'm not sure that is courteous," Juliet said doubtfully. "And it's so late."

Gil had gotten his stubborn look on him again, though. "Wasn't Sir Gawain supposed to ask about the sick man? That's in the joiners' play. You can check with Sir Eustache tonight, if you don't believe me." He sounded nettled. Then, not waiting for Juliet to write, he put a hand on the apothecary's sleeve. Raising his eyebrows to show his curiosity, he touched his own ear and lips, with a finger he then pointed toward the old man.

Juliet was relieved to see the kindly look that came to Jervis Towhee's face. He reached for the tablet once more, and changed it to say: **I YEVE THANKES FOR THISE GENTIL QUESTIOUN.** Then, rubbing that out, he added in small, quick letters: **I WAS YBORN YCURSED HETHEN. FADER MOORDRED EKE MODER. YIT BY HYS MAJESTIES TORTURE WAS I TAUGHTE**

TREW FEITH. He patted Gil's hand, then Juliet's. Then he reached under the counter once more and brought out a basket filled with wreaths of Midsummer herbs and flowers—verbena and daisies, meadowsweet and silvery leaves of mugwort. He put one on each of them, and patted their hands again. ❖

THE BOG

"I don't know—torturing a person seems a bad way to get him on your side," Juliet said. She and Gil were already well beyond the outskirts of Lincoln. They had crossed a boat canal, and the turns in the road and the rolling hills mostly hid the city behind them, except for the spire of Great St. Hugh. But they were still talking about the apothecary.

"Kings always do things differently than other folk do," Gil reminded her. "All the saints say we must be meek for heaven's will, and heaven it is that makes one man to be born a heathen and another a king. Besides," he added practically, "if a person cannot talk, he cannot complain about his father and mother being murdered."

"Did you see, on his throat?" Juliet asked. "I think he had a scar all 'round."

"From a rope, I trow," Gil said. "It's right mysterious."

Juliet felt a shiver at the back of her own neck,

though the sun had not set and the air was still warm. "Did I ever tell you about the leather man my grandfather found when he was digging peat?" Gil added after a bit.

"I don't think so," Juliet answered hopefully. Gil's expression at the moment was dead serious, but he didn't seem as sad as he had earlier. Lark was a good horse, but it was hard to pay attention to the pleasures of riding after so many hours of it in one day. How could it make one so tired to sit and be carried? "If it be an interesting tale, please tell it. And then I'll tell you one. How will that be?"

"I'd like that, Juliet," Gil said. Sometimes his manners were as gentle and courteous as if he were not merely a commoner. "It's a dark tale, I should warn you," he said. "Until it turns foolish. In truth . . . perhaps I should not tell it now, on Midsummer Eve before the bonfire's lit."

Juliet was torn. They *should* be sensible. There *were* the witches and greenycoats to consider . . . but Gil told such fine stories when he was in the mood—and she could see he was in the mood.

Fortunately, a good thought struck her. "Look. I'm wearing the brooch you made for me, with the holy relic of St. Ippolitt's shrine. That ought to keep us safe enough."

Gil actually smiled at her for a moment. "I *wondered* why you keep wearing that plain old thing," he said, "when everyone around you wears real jewels."

"I would wear it even if it were not from St.

Ippolitt's," Juliet told him. "Because . . . because it suits me." She didn't know why she didn't say *because you made it for me*. But she thought Gil was clever enough to know that. "Tell about the leather man. Was it some sort of doll?"

"Not it," Gil said, looking sober again. "It was a real man. Of some kind. Rather a short man, my grandfather said. Stark naked, except for his cap. And his skin all turned to brown leather."

Juliet shuddered and thought of the mummy powder in its tight tin box. But she wanted to hear more, and Gil kept telling.

"My grandfather thought, at first, it was some sort of brownie. But then he saw—it had a rope noose around its neck. And that's not all. . . ."

He had to stop talking for a moment. Argent had decided, for no good reason, to stop in the middle of the road. She stood, swiveling her ears as if there were something more to hear than the buzz of bees in foxglove, the *tchu-wu* of a house martin somewhere in the distance. Gil had to kick his heels into the jennet's side a couple of times before she moved again.

"A noose around his neck," he said then. "And in his hand—my grandfather said his hands were all shriveled and curled, and his nails grown out like a falcon's talons—he was still holding a wee loaf of bread, burnt hard as a rock."

"Saints bless us!" Juliet breathed. "What did he do?"

"He didn't do anything," Gil said. "He was dead."

"Not the leather man!" Juliet exclaimed. "Your grandfather!"

"Oh," Gil said, with a perfectly straight face. "Well, he went and told the priest. And at first the priest said twas an unholy thing, some criminal hanged for his sins, and they should bury him at the crossroads." He nodded, as if agreeing.

"Then Grandfather said, 'Lookee here, though, this bread's marked with a cross'—and so it was, like it were altar bread. So they thought, maybe twas some good man martyred for his true faith by the Danes, and they should bury him in the churchyard, so he could find his way to heaven easily.

"But then, Wat Atwell's grandfather, he was standing by, and he said, 'If he were a holy martyr, why did he not eat at least a bite of the altar bread for its blessing before they strung him up?'

"And then my grandfather said, 'How could he, with a rope around his craw?'

"So, by and by, they dug a hole half in the churchyard and half in the road, and they put the leather man in't, from the elbows down in the churchyard, because that was the half was holding the holy bread, and from his elbows up to his cap in the unblessed ground, because that was the part with the noose around it. And they took the wee loaf and sent it to the bishop, in case it'd do miracles. But we never heard that it did any," he finished.

"So he probably was not a saint," Juliet said. "But it's a curious story, anyway. I'm glad you told it."

They rode on a ways, companionably wordless, just thinking. By and by, it was Gil who spoke.

"Now, you tell one, Julie."

Juliet shook her head doubtfully.

"I could tell about King Arthur or Alexander the Great . . . but you already know all the stories I know," she began.

"Nay, that I do not," Gil protested. "You and Marguerite used always to be making things up. Tell one of those. Tell about the evil magician. . . ."

Juliet suddenly nodded decisively.

"Oh, Gil! I do have a new story! And it's not strange the way yours was, but it's strange, too. Listen to this odd thing I heard."

When she'd nodded, her daisy wreath had tipped over her forehead a bit too far, threatening to slide off. Juliet let go of Lark's reins for a moment and used both hands to settle the wreath more firmly in her hair, and then began with an explanation.

"Dost recall, we used to call the sorcerer 'Alsalabir' when we were playacting? Well, I don't really remember when we started, yet now I think we must have gotten that name when we were little from over-hearing Sir Pepin at table with his friends. And this is why I think it.

"When we were at Northampton last month, one day Marguerite and I were in the hedge maze amusing ourselves, speaking parts the way we used to, you know, at Rosebriar, pretending to be the good fairy Lisette and wicked Alsalabir.

"And we were thus play . . . we were amusing ourselves that way, and Sir Chester Knollys of Winchelsea
came up on the other side of the hedge all of a sudden
and roared out—you know how he roars!—'Who told
you Alsalabir was wicked? Show me the villain who
saith as much!' He sounded so overfierce—just the
way Marguerite and I used to make Alsalabir the
Magician act.

"You should have seen Marguerite. She was all
noblesse, perfectly brave. She did not show any
white feather. She said, 'Why, no one told us. It is
but a device of a child's fancy we discuss here, my
lord.'

"Then Sir Chester said, 'Forsooth, I'll hear no ill
of that name.' And then he told us this, his story.

"Alsalabir was a real and noble man, he said, a
Moor of Granada, where Sir Chester was shipwrecked
once. The boat he was on went down in a storm. He
said, when he had been in the sea for two days and
nights, there was no sign of his companions, nor was
there any plank or spar of the good ship to be seen.
He gave himself up for lost, and so he swooned away.
Yet by and by he awakened ashore.

"But there were two Moors there. One said, 'He is
from the north, let us kill him ere he recover himself
for to bear tidings to our enemy, the king of Castile.
For surely, this northerner be no more than a spy.'

"But the other, who was called Alsalabir, said,
'Nay, he is a fortunate man, for he hath paid the sea
enow, it wants no more of him. Let him come with

me to mine home, and I will ask him what marvels he
hath seen in his travels.'

"And so it was, for he took Sir Chester to a palace
where there were pillars of marble and steps of marble,
and marble statues of lions, and great urns with young
almond trees growing in them.

"And when Alsalabir brought him into that courtyard where those things were, all the white petals fell
from the almond trees so they lay like snow at their
feet. And Alsalabir saw Sir Chester Knollys stood there
in rags, so he sent for a white garment to put on him.
And he fed him well and gave him water to drink."

Juliet looked at Gil.

"You'll particularly like this next part, Gil
Falconer. That same day, Alsalabir took his falcons
hunting, and flew his lanneret at a magpie. And when
the magpie was cut open, there was a golden ring it
had stolen and swallowed.

"And when Alsalabir saw that, he thought it was a
sign to him to befriend this misfortunate stranger. So
he called a servant and had him bring a sack of gold,
and he gave it to Sir Chester. And every day they
walked together in a grove of lemons and oranges and
played chess together.

"But one day, near Midsummer, they were playing
chess and Alsalabir's servant brought him a cool drink,
with two ripe cherries in it. And one of the cherries
floated in the goblet, but one sank like a stone. And
then Alsalabir said to Sir Chester, 'My friend, I fear
for your life if I keep you here any longer for love of

your valor.' He made Sir Chester go to a certain town and to the dock there and find a certain ship and go away from that shore. And since Sir Chester had been out walking in the hot sun of that land, he was grown almost dark as a Moor of Granada, and his garment, too, was of Granada, and so he would escape unnoted from that heathen land.

"But when he was waiting by the dock, who should he overhear but that same knight who, with Alsalabir, had discovered him cast ashore. And the wicked knight did boast he had just come from Alsalabir's house, where he had killed Alsalabir for hiding a spy for the king of Castile. But the faithless knight did not look into Sir Chester's eyes that would have shown him the truth. Nor did Sir Chester have a sword to slay him on the spot. Yet it was with sore pity that Sir Chester Knollys sailed to Italy, and thence home to England, he said.

"And he said, 'A man can show no greater heart, nor more perfect hospitable love, than the Moor Alsalabir, for he laid down his own life to save and uplift a beggar at his doorstep.'

"And that is Sir Chester Knollys's real tale of Alsalabir."

"A good, round tale," Gil said after a respectful moment. "But I wonder, how could Sir Chester tell what the Moors said when they spoke?"

"We did not think to ask," Juliet admitted, "neither Marguerite nor I. Sir Pepin once told me, though, there are some Moors who can speak Greek and Latin as cleverly as the Pope's scholars. Perhaps Sir Chester learned when he went on pilgrimage to Jerusalem."

The sun had finally stooped below the horizon. The western sky was dimming into pennons of deep red-gold and violet. The east was a veil of deepest blue.

"Look!" Gil said abruptly. "Up on that hill yonder!"

Atop one of the wolds, they saw a wheel of fire flare up, then begin to roll bumpingly down toward someone's new-mown hay field. They could hear distant hurrahs and drumbeats, but it was already too dark to see any folks in the twilight. Jots of torchlight bobbed along the face of the hill, and that first flaming wheel disappeared in the shadowy valley.

"Where do you think we've gotten to?" Juliet asked. "How far are we, still, from Greenchapel?"

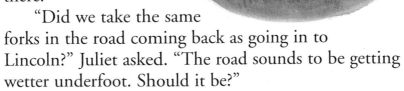

"We cannot be so very far, now. There goes another fire wheel! That must be Wragby House up there."

"Did we take the same forks in the road coming back as going in to Lincoln?" Juliet asked. "The road sounds to be getting wetter underfoot. Should it be?"

"Nay, by the saints," Gil answered ruefully. "These animals want their stable. I expect they've started us up some herder's lane that goes there more directly than the road does."

"Should we let them do it, then, if it's the shortest cut back?" Juliet asked anxiously. "I do not see how we can find the proper track in this little light. They'll be lighting the first bonfires soon, now it's dark."

"Look," said Gil, pointing out ahead of them, where a pale gleam showed in the distance. "That'll be the village at St. Cadmon's Well setting theirs alight. Wouldn't you figure it that way? Come on, Argent, pick up your feet. If this be the way, then, carry on. 'Tisn't far, now."

"Perchance we'll be there to dance by Greenchapel's own fires, then, after all?" Juliet hoped.

"Perchance," Gil said distractedly. "I have to go to the mews first, anyhow. I cannot go into the birds reeking of bonfire smoke, so I'll have to sift some of this mummy powder on Amfortas—and find Apple—before I can make merry."

"Let us hurry on, then," Juliet said with determination. She did not like to think about what ghosts or prankish spirits might be by the water on Midsummer's Eve. She did wonder if heathen kings' ghosts were like English ones, and might be forever trying to fetch their heads back from wherever they'd gotten to.

But she could tell that, just now, Gil was not even thinking of being afraid, only of how to get home.

On the whole, Juliet knew, Gil Falconer was of a fairly dauntless turn of mind—and, the saints knew, stubborn.

Lark and Argent clopped forward on the pebbly lane, their hooves occasionally splashing through puddles in the growing darkness. Insects began to chirr; cuckoos and night birds called to each other. Where the black line of the hills pressed against the blue-black sky, they could see torches nodding back and forth, and sometimes tiny swarms of what must be rushlights and lighted pinwheels. It seemed the bonfire at St. Cadmon's had not really caught yet—sometimes, folks were too eager, and loaded their fires with offal too damp or wood too green to burn well. Juliet sighed. The bonfire would have been a good beacon for travelers not familiar with the roads—travelers such as Gil and herself.

To stop worrying about that, Juliet started thinking about the Green Wolf Boys' play they'd been practicing all week. Jerome had made a rule that the girls could not watch it beforetimes. Even Jehan and Joseph had kept their parts secret. If she and Gil weren't back on time, she wouldn't be there to see them say their lines. Jerome and Aimery and Eustache would have the most verses to say. Or sing—she wasn't sure. All that was certain was that the evening would end with all of them dancing about the embers, running and leaping across the scarlet coals just as the fire began to show its first rich ermine of ash. *We are so close to Greenchapel now,* she thought. *I shall run into the ladies' quarters directly when we get there, and change to dry shoes for the dancing.*

A bit farther on, she noticed the lane had taken on a distinctly marshy smell.

"I like this not," Gil said after Argent had balked for the third time in twenty paces. He was some ways ahead of Juliet. "We are up-to-our-waists deep in water here. Where went that fire? It was our beacon."

"Are you telling me we're lost?" Juliet wailed.

Gil did not answer that. Instead, he shook his donkey's reins impatiently and chided her.

"Argent! Move!"

Argent moved. She staggered sideways and dumped Gil into the bog. ❖

CHAPTER FIVE

NOTHING DRY

"Gil!" Juliet cried. "Say something!"

"Where's my pouch?" Juliet heard Gil sputtering and spitting out bits of bog and shaking his wet hair back. "It was on my belt before I fell—it's in this muck. By the saints, that powder box had better be tight, or it's eleven shillings' worth of nothing."

"Gil," Juliet said firmly—frightened as she was—"you must get *out* of there! It's not *safe*." She peered into the failing light. Usually, she liked to think about elfen magic—but usually, it wasn't likely to happen to anyone she knew! What was that fluttering, off to the left? Oh, what if it was some watery fairy come to steal them? But, no; it was only a broken bullrush.

Gil was a shadowy form bending low over the surface of the black water. "My arms do not reach bottom, and my feet can't tell what they be touching, but it's warmish. I'll wager there's some leeches here. Julie, I've got to stick my head under, to bend low enow for my hand to find the pouch."

Juliet stared toward his quiet, reasonable voice. Off in the distance, fires flared here and there. She couldn't make out well which shape was Argent, which was Gil, which was clumpy, sodden plant hummocks. And what was that little impish shape? Only some grass?

"Nay, Gil, you dare not! Just leave it! That's what Marguerite would say."

"It's not what my dad would say. The gyr needs his medicine, and he needs it tonight. If that weasel bite has gotten infected in this high weather, there'll be no time to go back to Lincoln tomorrow to get another mummy's nose."

"I don't care about the beastly gyrkin!"

"Aye, you do, Juliet. A gyr with a bad wing cannot feed itself, let alone its master—he'd be as good as dead. I should not have said about the leeches" (and his voice had become teasing now), "but they'll be little, this early in the season, and I've plenty of blood. They might even be useful for working on Amfortas—"

"Stop it, Gil. Just stop it!" He had made her laugh, though.

"Juliet, this be nothing awful. I close my eyes when I put my head under, anyway. And this water's so clean, I could swim in't, if I'd a mind to. I only have to bend over once and touch my toes and what's right around them. My pouch just had all those shillings and the tin box in it, so it sank. But I'll get it. I'm only waiting to let the muck settle a bit." Then he said, "Don't let Lark move any closer. If this foolish donkey won't walk out of the bog altogether, I wish she at least wouldn't keep fidgeting around—hold still, you."

"What if I got her to come back this way? Would that help?" Juliet asked.

"If she'd go right back, and not tromp around my feet first. Don't get off Lark, though. Mind your new gown. She's not going to come to you, anyway. She's frightened of the bog—it's too soft under her."

"Argent!" Juliet coaxed. "Argent, come back here, come on, lass—oh, I know what!" Belatedly, she remembered the gingerbread in her pocket. Quickly she had it out and waved it in the direction of the nervous donkey. "Aye, that's it, back this way . . . come on. . . ."

Argent came over by Lark's shoulder now, snorting and dripping. Juliet made a grab for the jennet's halter before she let her get the gingerbread.

"Ah . . . aha. There! I've got her, Gil. Did you find it yet?"

"Nay, I must needs go under." There was a dull *splosh* in the darkness, lapping noises, and then a loud splash. "Got it, Jule! Is it still dry inside? Time will tell. Bag's tight, though." The darkness where Gil was standing filled with the invisible motion of his shaking his wet head the way Apple would. "*Now* what? Zounds! My boots are in the mud too deep!"

Juliet heard a few gulping, *slurch*ing sounds.

"I cannot walk in them, nor can I pull my foot from my boot. Hmm, now what?"

"Now," said Juliet, "I ride over there, you hold Lark's stirrup, we pull you out."

But Lark was as leery of the water as Argent had been, so Juliet ended up tying the jennet's reins to the palfrey's, dismounting, and wading over, herself, to where Gil was, to give him what help she could. The first thing she discovered was his herb wreath, floating where it had fallen from his head. She fished it out of the murk and put her arm through to carry it.

"Here," Gil said next. "Take the pouch and keep it from going in the broth again. If I don't need to worry about dousing it more, I reckon I can struggle out. There, that boot's looser than the other one. . . ."

Only a few moments more, and they were both mounted, feeling their way back toward the main road. Gil had only one boot on, and Juliet's gown would never be new again. They did not know if the mummy powder was dry enough to save Amfortas's wing. They did not know if there were any greeny-coats watching them.

At Wragby House, the Tailor's Company lit their bonfire with a wicker Big Man figure, but at St. Cadmon's Well there was no fire starting, nor ever had been. Only Will-'o-the-Wisp was abroad betwixt there and a certain bog that Midsummer Eve, misleading strangers and travelers.

Another hour had passed before they crossed the moat causeway at Greenchapel. True to his word, Gil insisted he had to take Lark and Argent back to the stable and go straight from there to the mews.

A heap of glowing coals was still smoldering just inside the causeway gate, where the Wool Guild had set their big basketwork St. John afire, and Gil bid Juliet jump off Lark there.

"Wish me luck, now, with that old buzzard, Amfortas," he muttered.

"Shall I come and help?" Juliet offered. Now they were finally back safe, it seemed odd to run off to the bonfire while Gil was still going about his work.

"Nay, I need you not. Two of us coming into the dark mews with a lantern would only wake him up more. Now I think on it, I'd best leech his wound before I put the mummy dust on it and rebandage him. Who can say—if I do it sweetly, perchance my mending his wing will make his stubborn heart mild to my wishes."

"You better take this," Juliet remembered, handing him his herb wreath she'd been carrying. He took it, but didn't set it on his head—it was still sodden. He look for a moment toward the west yard of the manor, where the festive noise of drums and flutes, strumming and shouting was loudest. He did not look sad, only thoughtful.

"Stand there where it's light. You don't look too badly soaked now," he decided. "And by daylight, when they can see you better, everyone's clothes are bound to be sooty." He grinned at her. "The falcons won't like many folk. Anyone whose bird bites, I'll get to exercise them—I might need help. If you don't get too smoky . . . If Apple's not back by now, I'll have to have a look for her, too." He stopped speaking for a moment then, and was more like he used to be at Rosebriar. "I give you thanks for your fair company all this day," he said. "And for reading and writing for me. Perhaps you could teach me to do it, too, when we have the time." He said it so softly, so lightly, Juliet was not sure if he meant it, or spoke it only as a jest.

But for once, Argent turned promptly, and trotted off toward the stable. Nor did Lark even try to tarry. ❖

C H A P T E R   S I X

BONFIRE LUCK

Juliet had given up her idea of changing her shoes. The rest of her was damp, anyway, and she could tell from the waves of laughter coming from the west yard that a play was being acted. She started to run, her shoes squishing at every step.

In the corner of the yard farthest from any of the buildings, the Green Wolf Boys had stood up a gigantic structure of poles and barrel hoops, painted and tricked out with greenery—a Jack of the Greenwood as tall as the rafters of the great hall at Rosebriar. In a cleared space in front of it, Jerome and Aimery, Eustache and Randall, and all the other Green Wolves were dancing a complicated knotting and unknotting of steps. They swung swords and hay sickles, leaping and stamping their right feet, which had bells at the ankles, and their left feet, which did not.

Juliet found Marguerite and Enid near the front of the flower-bedecked crowd, watching and clapping their hands with the music. Enid saw her first.

"Oh, Juliet, thank heaven you are safely home!" she exclaimed.

"I told you they would be," Marguerite said. "Though we were terribly worried when it got dark. But I said you and Gil together have enough sense to keep away from anything frightful." She hugged Juliet and added quickly, "But you're all wet!"

"Just bog water," Juliet said staunchly. "It will keep my new gown from getting holes burnt in it from sparks."

"You've had no supper, either, I trow," Marguerite worried. "Here, have this goblet of mead and milk—I only had a sip. There'll be Tom's gooseberry pudding later."

"That's Eustache in the helmet with the crown on it," Enid informed Juliet. "Their play is about King Edmund of East Anglia, and—the rogue!—he never let on that was why he was writing his new song!"

Indeed, it seemed the dance was coming to an end. As the last steps were finished, Randall Swynford, wearing a helmet with great horns on it, ceremoniously swung his sword at Eustache, and Eustache ceremoniously fell down on the ground.

Jehan and Joseph ran forward. They had quantities of fresh green leaves pinned to the hoods and tunics Juliet had made them, so they looked like little Jacks of the Greenwood, and they carried a basket full of more young leaves they dumped across Eustache's head and shoulders to hide them.

Jerome took up a torch and set it to the base of the giant leafy man. Little spots of light glittered at its feet for a moment—then, with a roar, leapt upward. Everyone in the crowd shouted out: "Long live the King!"

As the flames climbed into a great bonfire, the play went on. The Green Wolves made their speeches about Good King Edmund, his virtue and valor, and how useful his head had been to him and others. Eustache's arms and legs twitched about, very lively for a dead man's limbs. It was all very funny, and Juliet wished Gil were there to see it—especially since Eustache didn't seem to have any more lines to recite.

Then the Boys pretended to hunt about until Jerome supposedly found His Majesty's crown—with his head still in it. What he held up in front of the bonfire to show the crowd was an enormous, tough old cabbage. It had eyes—two chestnuts—fastened to it, and a mouth—a red stripe of bacon—and it wore a tin crown. Jerome held it up to his ear, as if listening to it whisper.

"He saith," Jerome explained, "that he be dead now." He listened some more. "He saith, let him only sleep for three days, and he'll be fine." Jerome the Wolf looked critically at the cabbage head. "Best make that, three months. . . ."

Whatever had been going to come next in the play, it never happened. All at once, there was a great writhing and commotion up atop the bonfire pile— and a dozen or more grass snakes suddenly wriggled

out of the shriveling greenery and, in their haste to
escape the fire licking toward them from below,
hurled themselves out into the yard all around.

The ladies shrieked, the men bellowed. Folks and
serpents scattered.

"That Randall Swynford!" Marguerite exclaimed.
"When he told me he'd collected a whole sack full of
snakes, I said I couldn't abide that old prank. He did
it anyway."

"Horrible!" Enid said.

"Hideous!" Marguerite
shook her head.

"But exactly what you'd
expect from Randall
Swynford," Juliet said. They
were all laughing. Juliet
wished Gil were there. Even
if he couldn't be in the
Green Wolves' play, he could
have enjoyed seeing it, frightened snakes and all. She would
have enjoyed it more, herself,
and so would have Marguerite. But
a gyrkin was a gyrkin, and to a falconer, that was that.

"Gooseberry pudding over by the kitchen," a servant shouted.

A bit later, Jack of the Greenwood collapsed into
a heaping bed of coals, and the Green Wolf Boys piled
more rubbish on so the fire leapt up once more. The
bolder men and boys began running and leaping

across its edges, showing how high they could clear it.

"Jerome and I danced around six fires already," Marguerite confided to Juliet. "This is the seventh. That should be good luck for our marriage. I want to have lots of children, like your mum."

The lines of dancers had begun to weave in and out of the crowd. Every time the song came to the two lines that repeated themselves, a couple would hold hands and run and leap the coals. Jerome, without his helmet, fetched Marguerite, and they whirled off. Then Aimery ran up to Enid and grabbed her hand, and they joined the line of "thread" looping through the ring of celebrants who were the "eye of the needle." Juliet found herself alone in the crowd, watching. Gil had still not come over from the mews.

Amfortas's wing must be very bad, Juliet thought. *I hope he didn't really go for Gil's eyes.* And, *I wish someone would come ask me. . . .*

Eustache and Peggy Swynford danced up to the needle's eye and ducked through, then ran and leapt across the embers at a low place. Peggy Swynford! So much for un-French lineage! Juliet thought Eustache could have done better leaping, but Peggy was too elegant to jump very high.

The farmers had begun to marshal their flocks, their pairs of oxen and their milk cows, to parade them through the billows of noxious black smoke. Harry, the stable boy, ran at the flickering coals and dove across, grabbing his cap at the last moment so it wouldn't fall off.

I reckon if I'm going to change my luck, Juliet thought regretfully, *I had better go leap across now, by myself, before the animals scatter what's left of the embers.* She sighed and ran—darted, like a falcon, into the smoke and out of it. Her wreath of daisies and verbena, meadowsweet and mugwort fell into the fire, where it was supposed to end Midsummer Eve.

When the girls finally trailed back to the ladies' quarters for their short night's sleep, Gil had still not come back from the mews.

Sometime between midnight and sunrise, all the sleepers in the ladies' quarters were awakened by a girl from the town of Malling. She was weeping and sob-bing, and madly pulling the pins out of her black for-tune-telling cushion. All she would say was, "All the doors in Malling had black crosses painted on them—but no one came. No one was there." The poor thing was almost hysterical with dream-grief, and Marguerite herself got up and made her catnip and camomile tea.

Juliet had never had time to make her own pin-cushion, but she had put a sprig of yarrow on her pillow. Sleepily she searched for it, and was relieved to see it had not wilted. That was good luck, a sign of true love. She could only remember a little of her dream, though—something about a falcon, about Mum gathering green strewing herbs. What Juliet held on to as she fell back asleep was the scent of Mum's herbs in the sleeping loft back at Rosebriar. ❖

MIDSUMMER AT GREENCHAPEL

"One for you," Enid said to Marguerite, and, to Juliet, "one for you."

The first thing all the girls always did on Midsummer morning was to run outside with their whitest, freshest kerchiefs to soak up the beautifying dew to use to wash their faces. Enid had just made Marguerite and Juliet gifts of exquisite cambric handkerchiefs edged with the daintiest lace.

"Oh, thank you, Enid!" Juliet said. Back in the old days at Rosebriar, she'd never had, or even dreamed of owning, anything so delicate. "It's like . . . it's like a petal!"

"And so shall be our complexions, if we go out now, before the sun's burnt off last evening's dew," Enid said briskly. Enid was always an early riser, but even when they'd dressed and made their way outside, Marguerite was still yawning.

"I never saw Gil last night," she remarked. "So many more folk were here than we have at Rosebriar bonfires. . . ." When she saw Juliet's face, she realized what had happened. "Oh—he had to take care of the baron's bird. I'm sorry, Juliet."

Perhaps if Marguerite had not been dancing all evening with Jerome, or even if Enid had not danced with Aimery quite so much, Juliet might have said something the night before. But she had not wanted them to stand aside with her, or to feel bad for her. She didn't now either, so she only nodded. She did not know what she could say. Of course, Gil had to finish his work for the baron before he could have fun himself. And, of course, she was younger than they were, and a commoner, not an heiress. No one expected she would be courted at this year's fire. She understood: They were her friends, even so. And Gil was still just her friend. And so was Eustache, for that matter—a friendly noble, not a suitor.

She said what Marguerite's old nurse, Beguine Clotilde, would have said brusquely, if she'd been there. "That's all right. This just wasn't my dancing night. This was my watching-my-friends-dance night. Another time, I'll dance."

But when the two older girls headed for the pear orchard, Juliet murmured that she'd find them later, and she lingered behind, looking about the courtyard. Serfs were already raking over the great black heaps of char where the bonfires had been, and the dung from all the farm animals brought in to make them prosper. The sunlight was pure and sweet and warm. Jehan and Joseph galloped by on their hobby horses, yelling gleefully. After all—here was another whole long day of Midsummer festival! Sugared berries, and white bread with juicy currants; archery contests, and music everywhere. . . .

"Good morrow, Juliet," Gil said, coming up beside her where she stood in the sunshine.

"Well met, Gil Falconer," Juliet said. "You sound merry, this Midsummer Day."

"Aye, that I am." He smiled on her. "I've already seen something that cheers me."

"Amfortas is getting better?" Juliet asked hopefully.

"Aye. We saved the old fellow. But I mean something better than that."

"Where'd you see it?" she pried.

"Down at the bottom of the garden."

"The garden . . . ?" Juliet had a sudden, absurd thought—childish, certainly, but still, she had to ask. "Gil, did you see Midsummer fairies?"

"Nay, something you'd a good deal rather see than a glimpse of fairies! Come with me, I'll show you."

He grabbed her hand, and they began to run—dodging first the people in the courtyard, then the lacy white elder bushes and borders of mignonette

and sops in wine along the overgrown garden path. No one was really watching, and it was a good run. In fact, it was such a glorious day, they were not even out of breath when Gil tugged her to a halt a few yards from the tangled hedge of pink roses.

Juliet felt for the relic from St. Ippollitt's, to make sure it hadn't come loose from her gown.

"Look, Juliet. Underneath it all," he said softly. He was holding aside a curtain of thorny stems.

There under the roses, the little red-gold spaniel, Apple, lay, watching them with her silky ears perked and her tail a wag. She was feeding two black puppies and three golden ones.

Juliet whispered to Gil, "It *is* better than fairies." ❖

MIDSUMMER CUSTOMS

During the Middle Ages, holidays marked the yearly cycle of planting, growing, and harvesting. In Juliet's England, even church feast days were often celebrated with customs from Druid and Roman times. The Druids' sacred mistletoe, oak, and evergreen, for example, were used to symbolize gifts from the heart, safety, and everlasting paradise.

Midsummer, the summer solstice, is the longest day of the year, so many of its customs featured symbols of the sun. Leaping bonfires and flaming wheels reminded people to be thankful for the blessings of growth and purification. On the practical side, bonfires—"bone fires"—were a way to clean up trash that

This William Blake illustration for Shakespeare's *A Midsummer Night's Dream* captures the spirit of Midsummer celebrations.

could harbor pestilence. The thick smoke would banish disease-bearing fleas, lice, and ticks from people and animals. The Black Death, a plague that swept across Europe later in the fourteenth century, was carried by fleas.

Midsummer was also the time of year when sheepshearing was completed and the first haying was begun: It was the first harvest, a time when folk planned for the future. Legends such as the story of Sir Gawain and the Green Knight recognized the "magic" by which green plants can be "beheaded" by mowing, and yet continue to live. Daylight, too, grew shorter after the solstice. In medieval art, St. John the Baptist was often shown wearing simple clothing made of sheepskin. He was said to have died by beheading, so the church celebrated his feast day at Midsummer.

The head of Tollund Man, some two thousand years old, is now permanently on display in Denmark.

Many scholars believe that in pagan times human beings actually were sacrificed to honor the sun.

Bodies of people who appear to have been ceremonially hanged have been found at different places in Europe. Gil's description of the "leather man" is based on the discovery of the Tollund man in a bog in Denmark.

Perhaps it was the long folk-memory of such terrible events, mixed with the breathtaking beauty of nature at Midsummer, that caused people to fear that mere mortals might be kidnapped then by elves, fairies, greenycoats, or other spirit-beings.

RELIGIOUS INTOLERANCE IN THE MIDDLE AGES

During the medieval period, many of the worst tragedies and injustices that befell individuals and nations were due to religious strife. Christians and Moslems alike, for example, believed it was their spiritual duty to struggle against unbelievers. Century after century, religious wars—crusades and jihads—set armies marching. Jews, pagans, and heretics, whose beliefs differed from society's mainstream, were the victims of cruel discrimination and persecution.

Granada, a kingdom in what is now Spain, was one of the last Moorish strongholds in western Europe. Sir Chester's description of the courtyard of Alsalabir is based on the famous palace called the Alhambra. The Moors and the Jews were driven out of Spain in A.D. 1492 by Ferdinand and Isabella, rulers of Castile and Spain.

"Great St. Hugh" of Lincoln was a bishop remembered for protecting the local Jewish community against anti-Semitic violence. Nonetheless, fifty years before Juliet's time, in A.D. 1290, King Edward I took over the property of all

The Jew's House at Lincoln still stands, but retains few of its original features, such as its arched door and window openings.

the Jews who would not become Christians, and forced them to leave England. In some cases, people were tortured until they agreed to be baptized.

The shop described as Jervis Towhee's is a surviving medieval dwelling known to this day as "the Jew's House of Lincoln."

READING MIDDLE ENGLISH

The notes Juliet and Jervis Towhee write to each other in Chapter 3 are spelled in Middle English, the language used in England in the fourteenth century. It is mostly a combination of Anglo-Saxon with the French spoken at court by nobles descended from William of Normandy—"the Conqueror." French was the upper-class language in which troubadours (and scholars such as Eustache) would have composed their poetic songs. The great English poet Geoffrey Chaucer (born around A.D. 1340) wrote his famous *Canterbury Tales* in Middle English. Many Middle English words look foreign to our modern eyes, but can be sounded out.

WHO SUFFRETH PEIN? Who suffers pain?

HOW GRETE BE HE? How great [large] is he?

FAT NU NOUGHT BRAWNY. Fat now, not strong [brawny, or muscular].

WHAT WILLE HE ETE? What will he eat?

JACKDAW HERTES, AND ELES AND MYS. Jackdaw (a small blackbird) hearts, eels, mice.

HYM LIKETH HYT NOUGHT. He doesn't like it.

HYT MAKETH HYM GRUCCHE. It makes him complain [grouchy].

HOW BE HYS COLOUR? How is his color?

ALLE WHITE FALLYNGE OFF FLESSHE. All [the] white falling off [the] flesh.

PRAYESTOW FOR MERCIE. [Prayest thou]; [You] Pray for mercy.

THIS MANNE DARSY BE A LEPRE. This man D'Arsy is a leper.

NOUGHT SIR PEPIN. Not Sir Pepin.

A WESEL BITEN OON HYS HAUKES. A weasel bit one of his hawks.

KEPESTOW DRYE THISE CURE. [Keepest thou]; [You] Keep this medicine dry.

WIR YEVE THANKES. We give you thanks.
I YEVE THANKES FOR THISE GENTIL QUESTIOUN. I thank you for asking.
I WAS YBORN YCURSED HETHEN. I was born cursed, a heathen.
FADER MOORDRED EKE MODER. Father murdered, also mother.
YIT BY HYS MAJESTIES TORTURE WAS I TAUGHTE TREW FEITH. Yet, by His Majesty's torture[r], I was taught [the] true faith. ❖

GLOSSARY

Amfortas *prop.n.*, in legends of King Arthur, the Fisher King, whose Wasteland kingdom was restored to order when Sir Gawain, seeking the Holy Grail, asks him how he came to be wounded

Argent *n., adj.*, heraldic French term for silver or white

cambric *n.*, fine linen fabric

coffret *n.*, small box, or coffer.

dost *v., 2nd pers. sing.*, do [you]

gyr, gyrkin *n., male* (female, gyrfalcon) *Falco rusticolus*, large sub-arctic bird of prey

heathen *n., adj.,* barbarian, uncivilized being

jennet *n.,* female donkey

joiner *n.*, a carpenter, especially one who does fine interior finishes (paneling, moldings, etc.). "Snug, a joiner" is a character in Shakespeare's *A Midsummer Night's Dream*

knot garden *n.*, flower and herb beds formally interlaced with walks; became very popular in Elizabethan (Shakespearan) period. When paths form a puzzle, it is a maze

lanneret *n., male* (female, lanner) *Falco laniarius,* small hawk found in southeastern Europe. The male is smaller than the female

leper *n.*, one suffering the disease of leprosy

Longshanks *prep., n.*, King Edward I (A.D. 1272–1307). Also called "the Hammer of the Scots." Grandfather of Edward III

molt *n., v.*, time of year when a bird loses its old feathers and new ones grow in; to shed feathers

noblesse *n.*, nobility (French)

nonce *n., adj.*, for the time being, for the present

saith *v., 3rd pers. sing.*, [s/he] says

show a white feather, phrase meaning "to act like a coward" or "to display poor breeding"

strewing herbs *n.*, aromatic herbs scattered on the floor to repel insects and perfume the house

stylus *n.*, pointed writing instrument

surcoat *n.*, outer coat or gown

swain *n.*, young man, especially one in attendance on a knight; a squire; a lover

wold *n.*, a hilly or rolling area of open country

Enter a whole new world of friendships and exciting adventures!

Juliet *Circa 1339*

Isabella *Circa 1820*

Kai *Circa 1440*

Marie *Circa 1775*

Shannon *Circa 1885*

GIRLHOOD JOURNEYS COLLECTION™

Share the adventures of the young women of Girlhood Journeys™ with beautifully detailed dolls and fine quality books. Authentically costumed, each doll is based on the enchanting character from the pages of the fascinating book that accompanies her.

- Join our collectors club and share the fun with other girls who love Girlhood Journeys.

- Enter the special Girlhood Journeys essay contest.

- For more information call 1-800-553-4886.

Ertl Collectibles™

Actual size of doll is 14".